# THE BLANKET SHOW

## Dandi Daley Mackall
### illustrated by David Hohn

WATERBROOK
PRESS

THE BLANKET SHOW
Published by WaterBrook Press
12265 Oracle Boulevard, Suite 200
Colorado Springs, Colorado 80921
*A division of Random House Inc.*

ISBN 978-1-4000-7205-7

Library of Congress Cataloging-in-Publication Data
Mackall, Dandi Daley.
  The blanket show / by Dandi Daley Mackall.
     p. cm.
  ISBN 978-1-4000-7205-7
  1. Bedtime—Juvenile fiction.  I. Title.
PS3613.A27257B57 2007
813'.54—dc22

                                        2007012102

Printed in China
2007—First Edition

10  9  8  7  6  5  4  3  2  1

*In memory of Bill Haberi*
     *—D.D.M.*


*For my Moon*
     *—D.H.*

Pick up the toys!

Grab your bear!

Got your blankie? Meet you there.

Kids are scurrying everywhere.

Time for The Blanket Show!

Shed those shoes.

Bye-bye, laces!

Everybody take your places.

Primetime, bedtime, bathroom races.

Time for The Blanket Show!

Curtain rising—such pizazz!
Bath-time boogie,
    Bubble jazz,
Scrub-a-dub and razz-ma-tazz!

Time for The Blanket Show!

Costume changes!
     You know how.
Jammies? Nightgown? Slippers? Wow!
Don't forget to take a bow.
Time for The Blanket Show!

Checking makeup?
You're all clear!
Funny faces, foggy mirror.
Toothbrush, toothpaste! Get in gear!
Time for The Blanket Show!

Bedroom scene,

   The setting's snug.

Jiving on the bedroom rug,

Nighttime jamming, jitterbug!

Time for The Blanket Show!

Tap dance fading,
 Soft shoe, too.
Ten-toed, barefoot boogaloo!
Jump in bed now.
 Peek-a-boo!
Time for The Blanket Show!

Bible stories are being read.
Fun to learn what Jesus said.
Snuggling, cuddling sleepyhead!
Time for The Blanket Show.

Intermission, don't you think?

Need some water?

    Just one drink.

Back to bed as house lights blink.

Time for The Blanket Show.

Moonbeam spotlight
on the stairs.
Balcony filled with
teddy bears.

Hugs and kisses. Say your prayers.
Time for The Blanket Show.

Curtain falling. Say "good night."
Heavy eyelids? Shut them tight.
Angels guard you through the night.
Time for The Blanket Show.

Go ahead and drift to sleep,
   Thinking,
      Sinking,
         Deep, deep, deep.

Count those fuzzy, furry sheep.
Time for The Blanket Show.

Last act of The Blanket Show—

Close your eyes and let it go.

Dream your dreams, for don't you know?

You're starring in The Blanket Show!